A Big Book of Jokes (500+) for Kids of all Ages

Paul Hill

Copyright 2023 Paul Hill

All rights reserved.

Cover by author.

Dedication

For Amelie and her friends
who helped me with many of the Jokes

And all those who have encouraged me including:

Laurence, Jo, Barbie, Alan, Jane, Brittany & Chris,
and Theo who would really rather just play tug-o-war!

Introduction

I have produced a few other books and some at least are a lot more serious than this. Having grown up with the humour of Monty Python, I always knew that if a book was supposed to be funny then it would have a joke in it.

I have tried to include some humour in all my books and there cam a time when I thought "why not compile all the jokes into one volume"? It wasn't quite as easy as it sounds but with the help of my daughter and some of her friends here it is.

While jokes are primarily meant to be funny, they can also be educational. For example, many jokes rely on puns or wordplay, which can help people learn new words and understand language in a more nuanced way. Jokes can also help people remember important information or concepts in a humorous way. Additionally, jokes can teach people about social norms, cultural differences, and the power of humour to bring people together. So while jokes may not be traditionally thought of as educational, they can definitely have a positive impact on people's knowledge and understanding of the world.

Paul Hill

March 2023

Jokes can be categorized in many ways, but here are some common categories:

One-liners: These are short, punchy jokes that rely on a quick and clever twist of language to generate a laugh.

Observational humour: These jokes are based on everyday situations or common experiences that many people can relate to.

Puns and wordplay: These jokes play with the multiple meanings of words or phrases, often resulting in a clever and unexpected punchline.

Self-deprecating humour: This type of humour pokes fun at oneself or one's own shortcomings.

Parodies and satire: These jokes mock popular culture, social norms, or political events in a humorous way.

Dark humour: This type of humour deals with serious or taboo subjects in a way that is morbid or unsettling, often eliciting a guilty laugh.

Physical comedy: This type of humour relies on visual gags or slapstick humour to generate laughs.

Insult comedy: This type of humour involves making fun of someone or something in a mean-spirited or sarcastic way. It can be funny, but it's important to be careful not to cross the line into bullying or harassment.

Needless to say, some of these categories above are more suitable for a joke book than others. In this volume we have a lot of puns and one-liners. I have steered away from anything dark as my intention here is that everything should be suitable for all. I've categorised them a little and have tried to focus only on those that are suitable for all ages.

Contents

Introduction 3
Animal Jokes 8
Camping Jokes 13
Chuck Norris Jokes 15
Clown Jokes 17
Colour Jokes 20
Computer Jokes 22
Crime Jokes 27
Dad Jokes 29
Detective Jokes 34
Doctor Jokes 38
Dog Jokes 42
Driving Jokes 44
Fantasy Jokes 46
Farm Jokes 48
Fish / Fishing Jokes 50
Food Jokes 52
Ghost Jokes 56
Holiday Jokes 58
International Jokes 61
Knock Knock Jokes 63
Military Jokes 70
Mystery Jokes 72

Observational Humour 74
One-Liners 76
Pirate Jokes 80
Riddles! 82
Robot Jokes 87
St Patrick's Day Jokes 88
Science Jokes 90
School Jokes 94
Space Jokes 98
Sports Jokes 101
Weather Jokes 104
For Python Programmers 107

Animal Jokes

How do you get a squirrel to like you?
Act like a nut

What do tigers have that no other animals have?
Baby tigers.

Where do you find giant snails?
On the ends of their fingers.

What do you call a deer with no eyes?
No idea. (No-eye deer)

Three cats are racing across the lake, one is called "Frank", one was called "Bob" and one was called "Un, Deux, Trois"
Frank came in 1st place; Bob came in 2nd place but Un Deux Trois never made it to the other side of the lake. What happened to him?
Un, deux, trois, quatre, cinq

Why are fish so smart?
Because they live in schools.

What did the fish say when it swam into a wall?
"Dam!"

Why did the baby elephant need a new suitcase for her holiday?
She only had a little trunk.

Why is a fish easy to weigh?
Because it has its own scales!

Why is a bee's hair always sticky?
Because it uses a honeycomb!

What do you call a parade of rabbits hopping backwards?
A receding hare-line.

Why aren't koalas actual bears?
They don't meet the koalafications.

What has 6 eyes but can't see?
3 blind mice.

What do you call an ant who fights crime?
A vigilANTe!

A turtle is crossing the road when he's mugged by two snails.
When the police show up, they ask him what happened.
The shaken turtle replies, "I don't know. It all happened so fast."

Why do birds fly south in the winter?
It's faster than walking.

Why do you never see elephants hiding up in trees?
Because they're really good at it.
I went into a pet shop. I said, "Can I buy a goldfish?"
The guy said, "Do you want an aquarium?"
I said, "I don't care what star sign it is."

A cop just knocked on my door and told me that my dogs were chasing people on bikes.
My dogs don't even own bikes...

What do you call a Camel with three humps?
Humphrey.

The baby rattlesnake asked its mummy "are we poisonous"?
The mummy rattle snake says "Yes, why"?
The baby rattlesnake says, "because I just bit myself on the tongue"!

What is the name of the Emperor Penguin?
Julius Freezer.

What do you call a hen who counts her eggs?
A mathemachicken.

Why don't oysters share their pearls?
Because they're shellfish!

What do you call an elephant that doesn't matter?
An irrelephant!

Why couldn't the pony sing a lullaby?
She was a little hoarse!

What did the buffalo say when his little boy left for school?"
Bison! *(bye son)*

What did the duck say after she bought chapstick?
Put it on my bill!

Why did the pony get sent to his room?
He wouldn't stop horsing around!

How do you make an octopus laugh?
With ten-tickles!

How do you keep a bull from charging?
Take away its credit card!

Why can't a leopard hide?
Because he's always spotted!

Why is a snake difficult to fool?
You can't pull its leg!

What's a cat's favourite dessert?
Chocolate mouse! *(mousse)*

What fish only swims at night?
Starfish!

What does a triceratops sit on?
Its tricera-bottom!

Camping Jokes

What do you call a camper without a nose or a body?
Nobodynose

What is a tree's favourite drink?
Root beer.

I went to buy a camouflage tent the other day.
I couldn't find any.

Why didn't the elephant carry a suitcase on his
Camping trip?
Because he already had a trunk!

Why do trees have so many friends?
They like to branch out.

A local farmer had opened up his land to campers. When I arrived, he helped me into the field with a wooden step over the fence.
I told him that liked his stile.

You can't run through a campsite. You can only ran…Why?
Because it's past tents.

Why did the camp warden quit his job?
Because it was so in tents.

Why are people who go camping on April 1 always tired?
Because they have just finished a 31 day March!

Did you hear about the kidnapping in the woods?
It's okay. He woke up.

Why don't mummies go on camping?
They're afraid to relax and unwind!

How do trees access the internet?
They log in

Chuck Norris Jokes

"Chuck" Norris is an American martial artist and actor. He is a black belt in Tang Soo Do, Brazilian jiu jitsu and judo. He starred in over 40 movies as a tough guy including the famous "Way of the Dragon" with Bruce Lee.

Chuck Norris doesn't do push-ups. He pushes the Earth down.

Chuck Norris can kill two stones with one bird.

Chuck Norris can unscramble an egg.

Chuck Norris can speak Braille.

Chuck Norris doesn't wear a watch. He decides what time it is.

Chuck Norris can win a staring contest against a brick wall.

Chuck Norris once got bit by a cobra. After five days of agonizing pain, the cobra died.

Chuck Norris can divide by zero.

Chuck Norris can set ants on fire with a magnifying glass - at night.

Chuck Norris doesn't flush the toilet, he scares the crap out of it.

Chuck Norris can strangle you with a cordless phone.

Chuck Norris once kicked a horse in the chin. Its descendants are known today as giraffes.

Chuck Norris once visited the Virgin Islands. Now they're just known as "The Islands."

Chuck Norris can sneeze with his eyes open.

Chuck Norris once had a heart attack; his heart lost.

Chuck Norris counted to infinity. Twice.

Chuck Norris can win a game of Connect Four in only three moves.

Chuck Norris doesn't read books. He stares them down until he gets the information he wants.

Chuck Norris can slam a revolving door.

Chuck Norris doesn't breathe air. He holds air hostage.

Chuck Norris doesn't call the wrong number. You answer the wrong phone.

Chuck Norris can kill a man in over 700 ways, with just his bare hands.

Chuck Norris can cut through a hot knife with butter.

Chuck Norris is the only person who can punch a cyclops between the eye.

Chuck Norris can lick his elbow.

Chuck Norris can make onions cry.

Clown Jokes

Did you hear about the clown who ran away with the circus?
They made him bring it back.

A friend of mine is an expert in making clown shoes.
It's no small feat.

Another friend has just got a steady job.
He's a tightrope walker in a circus.

What material is a clown's costume made from?
Poly Jester.

I had a friend who was a clown who performed on stilts.
I always looked up to him.

Saw a group of pheasants & partridges dressed as clowns.
I thought, "they're game for a laugh".

A friend worked as a trapeze artist until he was let go.

Why don't aliens eat clowns?
Because they taste funny!

Why did the clown cross the road?
To get to the silly side.

What do you call a clown who's always grumpy?
A frownie.

How do you make a clown cry?
Poke his funny bone.

Why did the clown refuse to eat the pizza?
it was too cheesy.

Why did the clown quit his job at the circus?
He was tired of clowning around.

Why don't clowns like to get wet?
Because it dampens their spirits.

Why did the clown bring a ladder to the party?
Because he wanted to raise the roof.

Why did the clown paint his face white?
He wanted to lighten up his day.

What did the clown say when he walked into the bar?
Why so serious?

Why did the clown wear a cowboy hat?
He wanted to be a rodeo clown.

What do you call a clown with a PhD?
A doctor of giggles.

Why did the clown bring a rope to the party?
He wanted to skip the line.

Colour Jokes

Why did the green pepper turn red?
Because it was ripening!

Why did the crayon go to the gym?
To get buff.

Why did the blueberry go out with the raspberry?
Because it couldn't get a date with the grape.

Why did the orange stop rolling down the hill?
Because it ran out of juice!

Why did the white dog turn red?
Because he saw the fire hydrant!

What colour is a burp?
Burple.

Why did the red car stop?
Because it saw the green light!

Why did the purple grape feel left out?
Because all the other grapes were in a bunch.

What do you call a lazy kangaroo? A pouch potato.

Why did the yellow bird go to the doctor?
To get a tweetment.

Why did the blueberry go to school?
To learn jammin' and jelly.

Why did the brown cow cross the road?
To get to the udder side.

What do you call a rainbow that's missing a colour? A "rainb."

Why did the orange go to the doctor?
Because it wasn't peeling well.

Why did the yellow paint refuse to go into the can?
Because it was too transparent!

What's black, white, and red all over?
A newspaper!

What colour is the wind?
Blew.

Computer Jokes

Why do programmers always mix up Halloween and Christmas?
Because Oct 31 equals Dec 25.

There are only 10 kinds of people in this world: those who know binary and those who don't.

Why did the server go bankrupt?
Because it ran out of cache.

What's the first step in understanding recursion?
To understand recursion, you must first understand recursion.

Why do they run Linux on the space station?
Because you can't open windows in space.

What do you call it when you have your mum's mother on speed dial?
Instagram.

Don't use "beef stew" as a computer password. It's not stroganoff.

I just got fired from my job at the keyboard factory. They told me I wasn't putting in enough shifts.

The cool part about naming a baby is you don't have to add numbers and a special character to make sure the name is available.

I bought a wooden computer, guess what?
It wooden work!

What do you get when you cross a computer with an elephant? A memory that never forgets.

Why did the programmer quit his job?
He didn't get arrays.

Why was the computer cold?
It left its Windows open.

Why did the computer go to the beach?
To surf the web.

Why did the computer go to the dentist?
It had a byte problem.

What do you get when you cross a computer and a snowman? Frost-byte.

Why was the computer wearing glasses?
It had lost its contacts.

Why did the computer go on a diet?
It had too many cookies.

Why did the computer get angry?
It had a byte to eat and no chips.

Set your Wi-Fi password to 2444666668888888.
So when someone asks for it, tell them it's 12345678.

What is the biggest lie in the entire universe?
I have read and agree to the Terms & Conditions.

Why was the computer so tired when he got out of his car?
Because he had a hard drive.

Why did Microsoft name their search Engine BING?
Because Its Not Google.

What did the spider do on the computer?
Made a website!

Autocorrect can go straight to he'll.

The oldest computer can be traced back to Adam and Eve.
It was an apple but with extremely limited memory.
Just 1 byte. And then everything crashed.

My Internet stopped working for 5 minutes.
Met my parents. They're nice people.

My laptop is missing a key. I lost control *(ctrl)*

How many symbols do you need to type on a keyboard to make a heart?
Less than three. (<3)

Why didn't the elephant use the computer?
It was afraid of the mouse.

I changed my password to "incorrect".
So whenever I forget what it is the computer will say "Your password is incorrect".

Somebody stole my Microsoft Office last week.
They are going to pay; you have my Word!

Why do most programmers use a dark theme while coding?
Because light attracts bugs.

What is an alien's favourite place on a computer?
The space bar.

My boss calls me "The computer".
Not because of my calculation skills but because I go to sleep when left unattended for 15 minutes.

I just got fired from my job at the keyboard factory.
They told me I wasn't putting in enough shifts.

What is it called when computer programmers taunt and make fun of each other on social media?
It is called Cyber Boolean!

What do you get when you cross a dog and a computer?
A machine that has a bark worse than its byte.

Crime Jokes

To the thief who stole my pillow, know this...
I will not rest until I find you.

I almost got caught stealing a board game today.
But it was a Risk I was willing to take.

What happens if someone steals uranium?
It becomes theiranium.

Why did the vegetable thief wet his pants?
Because he took a leek.

What kind of shoes does a thief wear?
Sneakers.

A man in Yorkshire has been caught on CCTV stealing police car tyres.
Police are reported to be working tirelessly to catch the thief.

Why did the burglar take a shower?
He wanted to make a clean getaway.

Why did the thief break into the bakery?
He wanted to steal some dough.

Why did the criminal go to the dry cleaner?
He wanted to launder his money.

Why did the criminal become a banker?
He wanted to rob people legally.

Why did the criminal become a politician?
He wanted to steal from more people at once.

Why did the criminal rob the bank on a hot day?
He wanted to get away with some cold hard cash.

Why did the criminal become a chef?
He wanted to steal the recipe for success.

Why did the robber take a bath before he stole from the bank?"
He wanted to make a clean getaway!

Dad Jokes

What do you call a factory that makes reasonable products?
A satisfactory.

What do Alexander the Great and Winnie the Pooh have in common?
Same middle name.

I only know 25 letters of the alphabet. I don't know why.

I asked my dog what's two minus two. He said nothing

What is the resemblance between a green apple and a red apple?
They're both red except for the green one.

I told my friend 10 jokes to get him to laugh.
Sadly, no pun in 10 did.

Why are Farmer's so cool?
They are outstanding in their field.

Can February march?
No, but April May.

Never criticise someone until you have walked a mile in their shoes.
That way, when you criticise them, you'll be a mile away, and you'll have their shoes.

Did you hear about the guitarist who fell asleep at a gig?
He had rocked himself to sleep!

There are II types of people.
Those who understand Roman Numerals and those who don't.

What is brown and sticky?
A stick!

I used to play piano by ear, but now I use my hands.

What do you call a bear with no teeth?
A gummy bear.

I'm reading a book on anti-gravity, it's impossible to put down.

What's the best way to watch a fly fishing tournament?
Live stream.

Did you hear about the guy who lost his left arm and leg in a car crash?
He's all right now.

I don't trust people who do acupuncture, they're back stabbers.

What do you call a fish wearing a bowtie?
Sofishticated.

I'm on a whiskey diet, I've lost three days already.

Why did the scarecrow win an award?
Because he was outstanding in his field.

Did you hear about the Italian chef who died?
He pasta way.

RIP Boiled water. You will be missed *(mist)*.

I used to be indecisive, but now I'm not sure.

Why don't oysters give to charity?
They're shellfish.

Why don't ants get sick?
They have tiny ant-bodies.

What did the grape say when it got stepped on?
Nothing, it just let out a little wine.

I'm reading a book on the history of glue, I can't seem to put it down.

I'm reading a book on the history of teleportation, but it hasn't arrived yet.

Why don't seagulls fly by the bay?
Because then they would be bagels.

I told my wife she was drawing her eyebrows too high.
She looked surprised.

Why did the coffee file a police report?
It got mugged.

Why did the old man fall in the well?
Because he couldn't see that well.

Why did the scarecrow win an award?
Because he was outstanding in his field!

Why did the belt go to jail?
For holding up pants!

What do you call a can opener that doesn't work?
A can't opener!

Why couldn't the bicycle stand up by itself?
Because it was two-tired

Why did the invisible man turn down a job offer?
He just couldn't see himself doing it!

How much does it cost a pirate to get his ears pierced?"
About a buck an ear! *(Buccaneer)*

What do you call a boomerang that won't come back?
A stick!

What did one hat say to the other?
Stay here, I'm going on ahead!

What's the difference between a hippo and a Zippo?
One is very heavy, the other is a little lighter!

Detective Jokes

Within minutes, the detective knew exactly what the murder weapon was.
It was a brief case.

What's a good name for a detective?
Mr. E.

A detective showed up at my house and asked me where I was between 5 and 6.
I told him I was at nursery school most days.

Why do detectives have such bad posture?
Because they always have a hunch.

How did the detective figure out who the railway engineer murdered?
He found his locomotive.

Yesterday, someone stole every single toilet from the local police station.
Today, detectives still have nothing to go on.

Detective one "I think the accountant did it, I found a calculator at the crime scene"
Detective two "That adds up"!

What do you call an estate agency opened by a detective?
Sherlock-homes!

What do you call a detective who solves cases accidentally?
Sheer-luck Holmes!

Did you hear about the detective who dropped his phone?
He cracked the case!

Why do ducks make great detectives?
They always quack the case.

Why do potatoes make such good detectives?
Because they always have their eyes peeled.

I couldn't believe that the highway department called my dad a thief.
But when I got home, all the signs were there.

Why do potatoes make good detective?
Because they keep their eyes peeled.

Why did the detective go to the zoo?
He was looking for the missing lynx.

Why did the detective go to the barbershop?
He wanted to trim down the suspects.

Why did the detective become a chef?
He liked to grill suspects.

Why did the detective go to the pet store?
He was looking for a purrfect witness.

And this 'detective' joke has been voted the best in the UK:

Sherlock Holmes and Dr John Watson go on a camping trip.

After eating their dinner around the campfire, they retire to the tent to go to sleep.

A few hours later Sherlock wakes up.

"Watson, are you awake?" He asks.

"Yes, sir. What is it?" Answers Watson.

"Look up and tell me what you see." Asks Holmes.

"I see billions of stars," says Watson.

"And what does that tell you Watson," asks Holmes.

"Well," says Dr Watson, "Astronomically, it tells me that there are millions of galaxies and potentially billions of planets. Astrologically, I observe that Saturn is in Leo. Horologically, I deduce that the time is approximately a quarter past three. Theologically, I can see that God is all powerful and that we are small and insignificant. Meteorologically, I suspect that we will have a beautiful day tomorrow."

"Why? – What does it tell you, Holmes?"

Holmes is quiet for a moment then says: "It tells me that someone has stolen our tent."

Doctor Jokes

Doctor, doctor, will I be able to play the violin after the operation?
Yes, of course.
Great! I never could before!

A man walks into a doctor's office. He has a cucumber up his nose, a carrot in his left ear, and a banana in his right ear.
"What's the matter with me?" he asks the doctor.
The doctor replies, "You're not eating properly."

Patient: "Doctor, doctor, I feel like a carrot."
Doctor: "Don't get yourself in a stew."

Doctor: "Nurse, how is that little girl doing who swallowed 10 coins last night?"
Nurse: "No change yet."

Patient: "Doctor, I've swallowed a spoon."
Doctor: "Sit down and don't stir."

Secretary: "Doctor, there's a patient on line one who says he's invisible."
Doctor: "Well, tell him I can't see him right now."

Why is a doctor always calm?
They have a lot of patients.

Patient: "Doctor, doctor, I've got a strawberry stuck in my ear!"
Doctor: "Don't worry, I have some cream for that."

How did the doctor cure the invisible man?
He took him to the ICU (intensive Care Unit)

Patient: "Doctor, my son has swallowed my pen. What can I do?"
Doctor: "Use a pencil until I come see him."

A man goes into the doctor's office and says, "Doctor, I've swallowed a watch. What should I do?"
"Take these pills," says the doctor. "They should help you pass the time."

Patient: "Doctor, doctor, I think I'm turning into curtains."
Doctor: "Pull yourself together!"

Patient: "Doctor, doctor, I feel like a dog."
Doctor: "How long have you felt like this?"
Patient: "Since I was a puppy."

Patient: "Doctor, doctor, I keep seeing into the future."
Doctor: "When did this start?" Patient: "Next Tuesday."

"Doctor, doctor, You've got to help me — I just can't stop my hands from shaking!"
"Do you drink a lot?" "Not really — I spill most of it!"

Doctor: 'You are very sick'
Patient: 'Can I get a second opinion?'
Doctor: 'Yes, you are very ugly too...'

Doctor, I'm having terrible trouble sleeping.
Try lying on the side of the bed. You'll soon drop off.

Doctor, Doctor, I only have 50 seconds more to live…
I'll be with you in a minute!

Why did the banana go to the doctor? It wasn't peeling well.

Why did the bird go to the doctor? It was feeling a little tweet.

Why did the doctor always carry a red pen?
In case he needed to draw blood.

Doctor, I need your help. I'm addicted to checking my Twitter!

I'm so sorry, I don't follow.

Dog Jokes

Once my dog ate all the Scrabble tiles.
For days he kept leaving little messages around the house.

What do you call a dog with no legs?
It doesn't matter, he still won't come when you call.

What's the difference between a businessman and a hot dog?
The businessman wears a suit but the dog just pants.

Why didn't the dog want to play football?
It was a Boxer.

Which dog breed is Dracula's favourite?
Bloodhound.

Why did the two-legged dog come to an abrupt halt?
It had two paws.

I asked my dog what's two minus two?
He said nothing

What do you get when you cross a Cocker Spaniel, a Poodle, and a Rooster?
A Cockerpoodledoo!

Why was the cat afraid of the tree?
Because of it's bark.

Why did the dog sit in the shade?
He didn't want to be a hot dog!

Why did the dog wear a bell around his neck?
He was a little husky!

What do you call a dog who loves bubble baths?
A Shampoodle!

Why did the dog join the circus?
He wanted to be a paw-former!

What did the dog say when he sat on sandpaper?
"Ruff!"

What kind of dog can tell time?
A watchdog!

Why do dogs make terrible dancers?
Because they have two left feet... and two right feet!

Driving Jokes

Why was the computer so angry when he got out of his car?
Because he had a hard drive!

What do you say to a frog who needs a ride?
"Hop in."

What kind of car does Yoda drive?
A Toyoda.

Where do Dogs park their cars?
In the barking lot.

I really need to get my car fixed.
Which car repair centre do you wreck-amend?

What do you call a Mexican who lost his car? Carlos.
What kind of car does a dog hate? CorVETS.

What part of the car is the laziest?
The wheels, because they are always tired.

What did one traffic light say to the other?
Stop looking at me, I'm changing.

Why did the car refuse to start?
Because it had a cranky engine!

What did the traffic light say to the car?
Don't look, I'm about to change!

Fantasy Jokes

Why do dragons sleep during the day?
So they can fight knights!

Why don't skeletons fight each other?
They don't have the guts.

What do elves learn in year one?
The "elf-abet"

What's the problem with an illiterate wizard?
He can't spell

Why do warriors fail in business?
They charge too much

What do you do with a green dragon?
Wait until it ripens!

What fizzy drinks do elves like best?
Sprite

Why do turkeys make good warriors?
Because they're not chickens

What is an incompetent wizard's favourite computer program?
Spell check

Did you hear about the skeleton who walked into a cafe?
He ordered a cup of coffee and a mop.

What do you call a dragon with heartburn?
Bad news for the nearest village!

What do you call a group of fairies that love to cook?
The sugar plum fairies!

What is a Vampire's favourite food?
A blood orange

Why didn't the skeleton go to the party?
He had no body to go with.

How can you tell a vampire has a cold?
He starts coffin!

What did Cinderella say when her photos didn't show up?"
Someday my prints will come!

Farm Jokes

What did the farmer call the cow that had no milk?
An udder failure.

Why did the pig have ink all over its face?
Because it came out of the pen.

If you have 15 cows and 5 goats, what would you have?
Plenty of milk!

Why shouldn't you play basketball with a pig?
Because it'll hog the ball!

What do you call a cow with no legs?
Ground beef.

What do you call a cow in an earthquake?
A milkshake.

Why did the pig dump her boyfriend?
Because he was a real BOAR.

What do you call a sleeping bull?
A Bulldozer.

What did the mama cow say to the baby cow?
It's pasture bedtime.

Why did the scarecrow win an award?
Because he was outstanding in his field!

Why did the farmer feed his pigs sugar and vinegar?
He wanted sweet and sour pork.

Why did the tomato turn red?
Because it saw the farmer blush.

I was having trouble with my internet at the farm, so I moved the modem to the barn.
Now I have stable Wi-Fi.

Fish / Fishing Jokes

Why are fish so gullible?
They fall for things hook, line and sinker!

What is the fastest fish in the water?
A motorpike.

What kind of music should you listen to while fishing?
Something catchy!

A monastery is in financial trouble, so it goes into the fish-and-chips business to raise money.
One night a customer knocks on its door. A monk answers.
The customer asks, "Are you the fish friar?"
"No," he replies. "I'm the chip monk."

Did you hear about the fight at the seafood restaurant?
Two fish got battered!

What did the fisherman say to the card magician?
Take a cod, any cod.

What is a fish's favourite show?
Name That Tuna.

Why did the fish blush?
Because it saw the lake's bottom

How do you communicate with a fish?
Drop it a line

Food Jokes

Where do you learn to make a banana split?
Sundae school

Why did the tomato turn red? Because it saw the salad dressing.

Did you hear the rumour about butter?
Well, I'm not going to spread it!

What do you call a fake noodle?
An impasta.

What did the girl mushroom say to the boy mushroom?
You're a fungi. *(Fun Guy)*

What cheese can you live in?
Cottage Cheese.

Where does Spiderman grill his burgers?
On his Weber!

Waiter, there is a fly in my soup, I think it's drowning!
No, it's doing the backstroke.

Why did the boy throw the butter out of the window?
He wanted to see a butterfly.

What did baby corn say to momma corn?
Where is pop corn?

Why did the banana go to the doctor again?
It was still not peeling well!

What do you get when you put three ducks in a box?
A box of quackers

Why did the cookie go to the doctor?
Because it felt crummy!

What is a table you can eat?
A vegetable

Why did the student eat his homework?
The teacher told him it was a piece of cake.

What do you call an avocado that's been blessed by a priest? Holy guacamole!

What's orange and sounds like a parrot?
A carrot.

How do you make an apple turnover?
Push it downhill.

What did the pecan say to the walnut?
We're friends because we're both nuts.

What did the baby corn say to its mom?
Where's my popcorn?

Why couldn't the sesame seed leave the gambling casino?
Because he was on a roll.

Why did the vegetable call the plumber?
It had a leek.

What do you call a band of berries practicing music?
A jam session.

What's a banana's favourite way to say "thank you"?
Thanks a bunch!

Ghost Jokes

What do you call a ghost detective?
An inspectre

What did the Ghost Teacher say to the class?
Keep your eyes on the board whilst I go through it again

What is a Ghosts favourite dessert?
I-Scream!

What room doesn't a Ghost need in his house?
A living room!

Where do fancy Ghosts go shopping?
A boo-tique!

How does a Ghost unlock a door?
Using a Spoo-Key!

How did the Ghost get from New York to London?
British Scare-ways!

Why didn't the Ghost go to the school prom?
It has no-body to go with!

Why are ghosts such bad liars?
Because they are easy to see through.

Why was the broom late?
It overswept.

How do you compliment a Ghost?
You look BOO-tiful

Holiday Jokes

What do you call Santa's helpers?
Subordinate clauses.

What do snowmen eat for breakfast?
Frosted flakes.

Why didn't Rudolph go to school?
Because he was an elf-taught reindeer.

What's the difference between a snowman and a snowwoman?
Snowballs.

What do you call an elf who sings?
A wrapper.

What do you get if you cross Santa Claus with a duck?
A Christmas Quacker.

What is a snowman's favourite breakfast food?
Ice Krispies.

What do you call a cat on the beach at Christmas time?
Sandy Claws.

Why did the snowman refuse to wear a hat?
Because he wanted to show off his bald head.

What do you get when you cross a snowman and a shark?
Frostbite.

Why was the snowman sad?
Because he had a meltdown.

What do you get when you cross a snowman and a vampire?
Frostbite.

What do you get when you cross a Christmas tree and an iPad?
A Pineapple.

What do you call an elf who runs away from Santa's Workshop?
A rebel without a Claus.

What do you get when you cross a snowman and a bulldozer?
A snowplough.

What do you call a snowman with a six-pack?
An abdominal snowman.

What do you get when you cross a snowman and a pig?
Frosty the Snow Hog.

What do you call Santa when he stops moving?
Santa Pause.

What do you get when you cross a snowman and a baker?
Frosty the Doughman.

Why was Santa's little helper depressed?
He had low elf-esteem.

Why did the turkey cross the road twice?
To prove he wasn't a chicken.

What do you call Santa's favourite pizza?
One that's deep-pan, crisp, and even.

What do you call a snowman in July?
A puddle.

International Jokes

What's the best thing about Switzerland?
I don't know, but the flag is a big plus.

how do you approach an angry Welsh cheese?
Caerphilly

How many Spanish guys does it take to change a light bulb?
Just Juan.

What do you call a Scotsman with diarrhoea?
Bravefart.

Sorry, love, can I have a pint of Guinness and a packet of crisps where you're ready there'.
'Oh. You must be Irish', she replied. The man was evidently offended and responded, 'The cheek, just because I order a pint of Guinness you assume I'm Irish.
If I ordered a bowl of pasta, would you that make me Italian?!'
'No' she replied. 'But this is a newsagent...

Why do French people eat snails?
They don't like fast food.

My mum set up a map in the kitchen, she told my brother that wherever the dart landed, we could go on holiday.
I guess that we are spending two weeks behind the fridge!

I asked my North Korean friend how it was there, he said he couldn't complain.

What do you call a man with a rubber toe?
Roberto.

Knock Knock Jokes

Knock, knock.
Who's there?
Boo.
Boo who?
Don't cry, it's just a joke!

Knock, knock.
Who's there?
Orange.
Orange who?
Orange you glad I didn't say banana.

Knock, knock.
Who's there?
Cow says.
Cow says who?
No, silly, a cow says moo!

Knock, knock.
Who's there?
Interrupting cow
Interrupting co—MOO!

Knock, knock.
Who's there?
Lettuce
Lettuce who?
Lettuce in, it's cold out here!

Knock, knock.
Who's there?
Weekend.
Weekend who?
Weekend do anything we want!

Knock, knock.
Who's there?
Theodore.
Theodore who?
Theodore wasn't opened so I knocked!

Knock, knock.
Who's there?
Robin.
Robin who?
Robin you, now give me my money!

Knock, knock.
Who's there?
Harry.
Harry who?
Harry up and answer the door, I'm getting cold out here!

Knock, knock.
Who's there?
Justin.
Justin who?
Justin time for dinner!

Knock, knock.
Who's there?
Tank.
Tank who?
You're welcome!

Knock, knock.
Who's there?
Hatch.
Hatch who?
Bless you!

Knock, knock.
Who's there?
Atch.
Atch who?
Bless you again!

Knock, knock.
Who's there?
Olive.
Olive who?
Olive you and I hope you'll be my Valentine!

Knock, knock.
Who's there?
Nana.
Nana who?
Nana your business!

Knock, knock.
Who's there?
Figs.
Figs who?
Figs the doorbell, it's broken!

Knock, knock.
Who's there?
Boo.
Boo who?
Aw, don't cry, it's just a joke!

Knock, knock.
Who's there?
Police.
Police who?
Police open the door; I forgot my key!

Knock, knock.
Who's there?
Alpaca.
Alpaca who?
Alpaca the suitcase, you load up the car!

Knock, knock.
Who's there?
Isabel.
Isabel who?
Isabel not working?

Knock, knock.
Who's there?
Ice cream.
Ice cream who?
ICE CREAM SO YOU CAN HEAR ME!

Knock, knock.
Who's there?
Icy.
Icy who?
Icy you in there!

Knock, knock.
Who's there?
Dozen.
Dozen who?
Dozen anyone want to let me in.

Knock, knock.
Who's there?
Scold.
Scold who?
Scold outside, let me in!

Knock, knock.
Who's there?
Water.
Water who?
Water you asking so many questions for, just open up!

Knock, knock.
Who's there?
Annie.
Annie who?
Annie body home?

Military Jokes

The Sergeant-Major growled at the young soldier: "I didn't see you at camouflage training this morning."
"Thank you very much, sir."

When I lost my rifle, the Army charged me £85. That's why in the Navy, the captain goes down with the ship.

The Pentagon announced that its fight against ISIS will be called Operation Inherent Resolve. They came up with that name using Operation Random Thesaurus.

What do you call a military officer who goes to the bathroom a lot? A LOOtenant!

Why didn't the troop tell anyone about their rank in the military? It was PRIVATE.

What is a Soldier's least favourite month? MARCH!

The sergeant asked, "Corporal, why did you salute that tiger?"
The corporal replies, "Didn't you see all his stripes?"

A cookie and a piece of cake joined the army, but eventually, they abandoned their fellow soldiers. Now, they are wanted for dessertion.

Where does the General keep his armies?
In his sleevies!

Why did the soldier go to art school?
He wanted to learn how to draw his weapon!

Mystery Jokes

How many mystery writers does it take to change a light bulb?
Two. One to change the bulb, and the other to give it an unexpected twist at the end.

I'm thinking of writing a mystery novel.
Or am I?

What do you call a group of racist chickens playing mystery board games?
A Clue Clucks Clan

The mystery of how my luggage works has been solved.
It was an open and shut case.

Some mystery person keeps adding soil to my garden.
The plot thickens.

There was a mystery involving an office worker and a small bag.
It was a brief case.

I watched a murder mystery movie with my daughter. She said, "Hey! They just stole this idea from Among Us!"

what do you call a group of crows and a dead one
a murder mystery (a group of crows is called a murder)

How many mystery writers does it take to change a light bulb?
Two. One to change the bulb, and the other to give it an unexpected twist at the end.

They say it's a mystery how the pyramids were built. But it seems obvious to me - they probably started at the bottom and worked their way up.

There was a mystery involving an office worker and a small bag.
It was a brief case.

Observational Humour

I went to a bookstore and asked the saleswoman
where the self-help section was.
She said if she told me, it would defeat the purpose.

Why do they lock gas station bathrooms?
Are they afraid someone will clean them?

Why do we park in driveways and drive on parkways?

I always wondered why somebody doesn't do
something about that.
Then I realized I was somebody.

I told my wife she was drawing her eyebrows too high.
She looked surprised.

I'm not a vegetarian because I love animals.
I'm a vegetarian because I hate plants.

Why is it that when we talk to God, we're praying, but
when God talks to us, we're schizophrenic?

I have a photographic memory.
But I always forget to take the lens cap off.

I saw a sign that said 'Watch for children' and I
thought, 'That sounds like a fair trade'.

I love airports because the rules of society don't apply. You can eat a sandwich for breakfast, a pizza for lunch, and a hamburger for dinner, and nobody judges you.

I hate when I think I'm buying organic vegetables, and when I get home I discover they're just regular donuts.

I wish I could turn back the clock. I'd find whoever invented the snooze button and punch them in the face.

I went to a restaurant that serves breakfast at any time. So I ordered French Toast during the Renaissance.

I love the sound of birds singing early in the morning, as long as they're singing somewhere far away and not in a tree outside my window.

I hate when I go to shake someone's hand and they give me the dead fish.
It's like they're saying, 'I don't care about making a good impression'.

I don't understand why people say 'life is short.' Life is actually the longest thing you'll ever experience.
It's death that's short.

One-Liners

I'm reading a book on anti-gravity. It's impossible to put down.

I used to play piano by ear. Now I use my hands.

I used to be indecisive. Now I'm not sure.

I'm addicted to brake fluid. But I can stop anytime.

I told my wife she was drawing her eyebrows too high. She looked surprised.

I'm a big fan of whiteboards. They're re-markable.

I'm on a whisky diet. I've lost three days already.

I told my wife she was overreacting. She just rolled her eyes and walked away. That's a strange way to start a conversation.

I used to be a baker, but I couldn't make enough dough.

I have a photographic memory. But I always forget to take the lens cap off.

I used to be a baker, but I couldn't raise the dough.

I'm a terrible cook, but I'm good at ordering takeout.

I'm so old, I remember when emojis were called hieroglyphics.

I'm reading a book about anti-gravity. It's impossible to put down.

What has four wheels and flies?"
A garbage truck!

I used to be a lifeguard, but some blue kid got me fired.

I used to be a banker, but I lost interest.

I'm not arguing, I'm just explaining why I'm right.

I told my wife she was painting her living room the wrong colour. She said, 'who's living in it, you or me?'

I used to be a professional baker, but then I kneaded dough.

I'm reading a book about teleportation. It's bound to have its ups and downs.

I'm not arguing, I'm just passionately expressing my obvious superiority.

I'm a perfectionist with a procrastination problem.

I'm so bad at cooking, my smoke alarm goes off when I make toast.

I hate when people steal my ideas, but I love it when they make them better.

I tried to make a belt out of watches, but it was a waist of time.

I'm a self-made millionaire. I just didn't have any help from anyone else.

I have a degree in liberal arts. Do you want fries with that?

I tried to start a hot air balloon business, but it never took off.

I'm not lazy, I'm energy efficient.

I'm not short, I'm just concentrated awesome.

I'm a big fan of whiteboards. I find them quite remarkable.

I don't trust people who don't like dogs, but I always trust a dog when it doesn't like a person.

I used to be in a band called 'The Prevention.' We never got a gig.

I have the memory of a goldfish. Every time I hear a joke, it's like the first time.

I'm so bad at math, I couldn't count the number of times I've failed.

I once saw a movie about how ships are kept together. It was riveting.

Pirate Jokes

Why are Pirates called Pirates? Because they arrrrr!

Why don't Pirates take a shower before they walk the plank?
They just wash up on shore.

What is a Pirates favourite doll?
BAAAAARRRRBIE!

Why did the pirate buy an eye patch?
Because he couldn't afford an iPad!

What do Pirates wear in the winter?
Long Johns!

What's a Pirates favourite part of a song?
The hook!

What do you call a pirate who steals from the rich and gives to the poor?
Robin Hook!

What do you call a stupid pirate?
The pillage idiot!

Why couldn't the Pirates play cards?
Because the captain was standing on the deck!

How do Pirates like to cook their steaks?
On a BAAAARRRRRBECUE!

What happens if you take the p out of a pirate?
He becomes irate!

What do you call a pirate with three eyes?
Piiirate!

Why does it take Pirates so long to learn the alphabet?
Because they can spend years at C!

How did the pirate find out he needed glasses?
He took an aye exam!

What's a Pirates favourite type of music?
Rum & Bass!

How do Pirates know they exist?
They think, therefore they ARRRRRRR!!!

Riddles!

What has two hands and a face, but no arms and legs?
A clock.

What is the longest word in the English language?
SMILES: there is a mile between the first and last letters!"

What has a neck, but no head?
A bottle.

Where is the ocean the deepest?
On the bottom.

When does the (English) alphabet have only 25 letters?
At Christmas time, because it is the time of Noel

What gets wetter as it dries?
A towel

Why did the tomato blush?
Because it saw the salad dressing!

How far can a dog run into the forest?
Halfway, after that he is running out of the forest.

There were some twins. One was twenty, the other was twenty 2. One married the other. How can be this ?
One was twenty, the other twenty too. One was a vicar so he married the other

How many people are buried in that cemetery?
All of them.

Why don't we need a compass at the North Pole?
Because every direction is south.

What is as big as a horse but doesn't weigh anything?
The horse's shadow.

Which room has no doors, no windows.
A mushroom.

What are the two strongest days of the week?
Saturday and Sunday. All the others are weekdays.

What is full of holes but still holds water?
A sponge.

What is always in front of you but can't be seen?
The future.

How does a river say hello?
It waves.

What can only live if there is light but dies if the light shines on it?
A shadow

What goes up but never goes down?
Your age

What is always in front of you but can't be seen?
The future.

What has a heart that doesn't beat?
An artichoke.

What has a neck but no head?
A bottle.

What has a thumb and four fingers but is not a hand?
A glove.

What has a head and a tail but no body?
A coin.

What is full of holes but still holds water?
A sponge.

What is always in bed but never sleeps?
A river.

I have cities, but no houses. I have mountains, but no trees. I have water, but no fish. What am I?
A map.

What has four legs in the morning, two legs in the afternoon, and three legs in the evening?
A human. They crawl on all fours as a baby, walk on two legs as an adult, and use a cane in old age.

The more you take, the more you leave behind. What am I?
Footsteps.

I am not alive, but I grow; I don't have lungs, but I need air; I don't have a mouth, but I need water to survive. What am I?
Fire.

What begins with T, ends with T, and has T in it?
A teapot.

What is always in front of you but can't be seen?
 The future.

I am light as a feather, yet the strongest man cannot hold me for much more than a minute. What am I?
Breath.

I am always hungry, I must always be fed. The finger I touch, will soon turn red. What am I?
Fire.

What goes through cities and fields, but never moves?
A road.

I am an odd number. Take away a letter and I become even. What number am I?
Seven.

What can you catch but not throw?
A cold.

Robot Jokes

What happens to robots after they go defunct?
They rust in peace!

Why do robots make bad teachers?
They just drone on and on!

What do you call a robot who likes to row?
A row-bot!

How do robots pay for things?
With cache, of course!

Why did the robot fail his exam?
He was a bit rusty!

Why did the robot get upset?
Because everyone was pushing his buttons!

Why are some robots insecure?
Because their intelligence is artificial!

What is a robot's favourite dance move?
The human.

St Patrick's Day Jokes

Why did the leprechaun go outside?
To sit on his paddy-o

What type of bow cannot be tied?
A rainbow

What is a leprechaun's favourite type of music?
Sham-rock 'n' roll

What do ghosts drink on St. Patrick's Day?
BOOs *(booze)*

What do you call an Irish spider?
Paddy long legs

When does a leprechaun cross the street?
When it turns green

What would you get if you crossed Christmas with St. Patrick's Day?

St. O'Claus

What did the leprechaun say when the video game ended?

Game clover

What did one Irish ghost say to the other?

Top O' the moaning to you

What do you call a fake Irish diamond?

A shamrock

Science Jokes

Why did the electron go to the doctor?
Because it had a proton.

What did the scientist say when he found two isotopes of helium?
HeHe.

Why did the chicken cross the Mobius strip?
To get to the same side.

Why did the physicist break up with his girlfriend?
She had too much potential.

Why do chemists like nitrates so much?
They're cheaper than day rates.

Why did the bacteria cross the road?
To get to the other slide.

What did the physicist say when he got arrested?
I'm charged with crimes against gravity.

Why do scientists enjoy working with acids?
Because they like to pH test.

How many quantum physicists does it take to change a light bulb?
Two: one to change it and one to observe how it behaves differently in the presence of an observer.

What do you get when you cross a snowman and a shark? Frostbite.

Why was the science book sad?
Because it had too many problems.

Why don't bacteria go to movies?
They can't afford the popcorn.

Why did the computer go to the doctor?
Because it had a virus.

How do you know when a joke is a "dad joke"?
It becomes apparent.

Why do chemists like to work with ammonia?
Because it's pretty basic.

Why did the chemist break up with his girlfriend?
She said he was too basic.

Why did the physics teacher break up with her boyfriend?
He just didn't understand her attraction.

What do you call an alligator in a lab coat?
An investigator.

Why did the atom cross the road? To get to the other side.

Why do chemists call helium, curium, and barium "the medical elements"?
Because if you can't heal-ium or cure-ium, you barium!

How do you know when a joke is a "dad joke"?
When the punchline is apparent. *(a parent)*

Why did the physicist put salt on his pizza?
To decrease the uncertainty.

What did the DNA say to the other DNA?
Do these genes make me look fat?

Why did the scientist cross the road?
To get to the other hypothesis.

Why did the chemist keep a journal?
To keep track of his ex-periments.

Why did the physicist break up with the biologist?
There was no chemistry.

Two atoms were walking down the street, one suddenly said, "I think I lost an electron." The other asked, "Are you positive?"

Did you hear about the mathematician who's afraid of negative numbers? He'll stop at nothing to avoid them.

Did you hear about the geologist who was reading a book about Helium? He couldn't put it down!

I asked the guy sitting next to me if he had any Sodium Hypobromite. He said NaBrO.

School Jokes

Why did the music teacher need a ladder? To reach the high notes

What's the worst thing you're likely to find in the school cafeteria?
The Food!

Why did nose not want to go to school?
He was tired of getting picked on!

What happened when the wheel was invented?
It caused a revolution!

Why was school easier for cave people?
Because there was no history to study!

David comes home from his first day of school, and his mother asks, "What did you learn today?"
"Not enough," David replies. "They said I have to go back tomorrow."

Why did the M&M go to school? Because he really wanted to be a Smartie!

Why was the teacher wearing sunglasses to school?
She had bright students!

Johnny: "Would you punish me for something I didn't do?"
Teacher:" Of course not."
Johnny: "Good, because I haven't done my homework."

Teacher: Do you have trouble making decisions?
Pupil: Well...yes and no.

Teacher: Did your father help you with your homework?
Pupil: No, he did it all by himself.

How do you keep warm in a cold room?
You go to the corner because it's always 90 degrees.

Why is it sad that parallel lines have so much in common?
Because they'll never meet.

Why can't a nose be 12 inches long?
Because then it would be a foot.

Why did the student get upset when her teacher called her average?
It was a "mean" thing to say!

Why was six afraid of seven?
Because seven, eight, nine!

How do you make seven an even number?
Just remove the "s!"

There are three kinds of people in this world.
Those who can count and those who can't.

Why did the math book look sad?
Because it had too many problems.

Why don't scientists trust atoms?
Because they make up everything.

Why did the history teacher go to the beach?
To teach the class about the sunken ships.

Why did the teacher give the class a compass?
To make sure they were headed in the right direction.

Why did the music teacher need a ladder?
To reach the high notes.

Why did the student eat his homework?
Because his teacher said it was a piece of cake.

What do you get when you cross a snowman and a shark?
Frostbite.

Why was the math book sad? Because it had too many problems.

What is a math teacher's favourite dessert?
Pi

What happened when the world's tongue-twister champion got arrested?
They gave him a tough sentence!

3.14% of sailors are Pi Rates.

Space Jokes

What was the first animal in space?
The cow that jumped over the moon!

What did Mars say to Saturn?
Give me a ring sometime.

Learning about space all day is exhausting.
I need a launch break.

Orion's Belt is a huge waist of space.

I want to be an astronaut when I grow up but my mum says I have high hopes.

Astronauts are the only people who keep their jobs after they get fired

A pair of twins decided on adventurous careers.
One became an astronaut.
The other became a skydiver. He was more down to earth.

How do you throw a space party?
You planet.

Why didn't people like the restaurant on the moon?
Because there was no atmosphere.

How do you get a baby astronaut to go to sleep?
You Rocket.

Why did the astronaut break up with her boyfriend?
Because she needed some space.

Why don't aliens eat clowns?
Because they taste funny!

What did the alien say to the garden?
Take me to your weeder!

What did the alien say to the gas pump?
Take your finger off the trigger, Earthling.

Why did the sun go to school?
To get brighter.

What did one astronaut say to the other before launching into space?
I'm over the moon to be here.

What do you call a group of astronauts that performs on stage? A constellation.

Why did the robot go on a diet?
Because he had too many empty calories.

How do you organize a space party? You planet.

Why do astronauts always break up before they go into space? They just need their space.

Why don't aliens eat clowns? Because they taste funny.

What do you call an alien with no ears? Whatever you want, he can't hear you.

Why did the alien refuse to eat the astronaut? He said he tasted a little meteor than he was used to.

Where should a 500-pound alien go?
On a diet!

Sports Jokes

Why do Golfers carry an extra pair of socks?
In case they get a hole in one!

Why should you never date a tennis player?
Love means nothing to them.

I was in the gym earlier and decided to jump on the treadmill. People were giving me weird looks, so I started jogging instead.

Why did the golfer wear two pairs of pants?
In case he got a hole in one.

I asked my date to meet me at the gym today.
She didn't show up.
That's when I knew we weren't going to work out.

What runs around a football field but never moves?
A fence.

What kind of tea do football players drink?
Penaltea.

What's the difference between a poorly dressed man on a bicycle and a nicely dressed man on a tricycle?
A tyre. (Attire!)

Why did the baseball team hire a detective? To find their missing pitcher.

Why do basketball players love donuts? Because they like to dunk them.

Why did the soccer player bring string to the game? So he could tie the score.

What did the baseball glove say to the ball? "Catch you later!"

Why was the basketball court always wet? Because the players kept dribbling.

Why was the baseball stadium so cold? Because there were a lot of fans.

Why did the basketball player bring a ladder to the game? He wanted to shoot for the stars.

American Football Jokes

Why did the football coach go to the bank?
To get his quarter back.

Why was the tiny ghost asked to join the football team?
They needed a little team spirit.

Which football player wears the biggest helmet?
The one with the biggest head.

Why did Cinderella get kicked out of the football team?
Because she kept running away from the ball!

Why are college football stadiums always cool?
Because they're full of fans.

Why did the chicken get ejected from the football game?
For persistent fowl play.

What did the football player say to the vending machine?
Give me my quarterback!

Weather Jokes

What's the difference between weather and climate?
You can't weather a tree, but you can climate.

How do you prevent a summer cold?
Catch it in the winter.

How do hurricanes see?
With one eye!

What does a cloud wear under his raincoat?
Thunderwear.

What type of lightning likes to play sports?
Ball lightning.

What did one lightning bolt say to the other?
"You're shocking!"

What did the tornado say to the sports car?
"Want to go for a spin?"

When are your eyes not eyes?
When the cold wind makes them water!

What's a tornado's favourite game?
Twister!

What did one volcano say to the other?
"I lava you."

What falls but never hits the ground?
The temperature.

What does everyone listen to, but no one believes?
A weather reporter.

What is the opposite of a cold front?
A warm back.

Why is the sun so smart?
It has over 5,000 degrees.

What do you call it when it's pouring ducks and geese?
Fowl weather!

What is the best day to go to the beach?
Sun-day, of course.

And one of the most famous jokes, often purported to be true but more likely an urban legend:

This is the transcript of a radio conversation of a US naval ship with Canadian authorities off the coast of Newfoundland in October 1995. Radio conversation released by the Chief of Naval Operations 10-10-95.

Americans: Please divert your course 15 degrees to the North to avoid a collision.

Canadians: Recommend you divert YOUR course 15 degrees to the South to avoid a collision.

Americans: This is the Captain of a US Navy ship. I say again, divert YOUR course.

Canadians: No. I say again, you divert YOUR course.

Americans: This is the aircraft carrier USS Lincoln, the second largest ship in the United States' Atlantic fleet. We are accompanied by three destroyers, three cruisers and numerous support vessels. I demand that YOU change your course 15 degrees north, that's one five degrees north, or countermeasures will be undertaken to ensure the safety of this ship.

Canadians: This is a lighthouse. Your call.

For Python Programmers

Are you a Python programmer? (see my other books).

If you are and you need more jokes, why not get help from Python?

If you have Python installed on your computer then install pyjokes:
pip install pyjokes

and then in Python a tiny bit of code like this:

```
import pyjokes
my_joke = pyjokes.get_joke() # get a random joke
print(my_joke)
```

Will provide access to a library of hundreds more jokes...

And if you have time, why not create a Python GUI that produces jokes at the press of a button? If you don't know how, take a look at my other books.

The End

Please watch out for my next book!